I Am Cancer

Lisa R. Perron

LITTLE RED HOUSE
PUBLISHING

TABLE OF CONTENTS

CHAPTER ONE

"Isn't it ironic that I was the one who wanted the divorce and you're the one who ends up happy?" I ask David while standing in the doorway of my small two-bedroom bungalow, watching his newest girlfriend help our two young daughters into the car.

"Who says I'm happy?" The right side of David's mouth lifts a little. I always thought that crooked smile of his was sexy. Still do, I guess. The expression always reveals David's vulnerability and a tenderness that he didn't often let show—at least not for a while. I wonder if he ever smiles that way for the skinny blond currently leaning into his car to buckle our youngest, Charlotte, into her car seat.

My chest is heavy with disappointment and jealously as the realization of David's intimacy with this woman hits. Woman, ha— she's basically a girl.

"You're not happy?" I ask. The idea is absurd to me. How could he not be happy with Trish—or is it Tracy? For some reason, I can't recall this one's name. My stomach clinches with guilt. How can I let my daughters leave with a woman whose name I can't remember?

David smiles—a full, both sides of his mouth smile—and says, "I didn't say that."

Mind games. *This is why I'm not married to David anymore*, I tell myself. Except that I know that it's not true. I'm not sure why I ended our marriage. David wasn't abusive or unfaithful. There really isn't anything terribly wrong with his character. I just wasn't happy, and I was sure it was because I had chosen the wrong man to grow old with.

I stare at David, trying to detect whether he is telling me the truth. A part of me hopes that he is just as miserable as me, and the other part feels guilty about it. I should want him to be happy, shouldn't I? I look away to see beautiful what's-her-name leaning against the car smiling as us. She raises a perfectly manicured hand and bends her elegant fingers in a wave. I actually don't know what her nails look like because I can't see them from here. Maybe she chews them off. The thought of that makes me smile.

"Thanks for keeping the girls for me tomorrow."

"Thank you for letting me have them again on an unscheduled day," he says, and I can tell he means it. "Meredith and I are going to take them to the new water park over on Elm Street."

My heart jumps to my throat. I wanted to be the first one to take Emmie and Charlotte there. But, I've had all summer to make it happen and didn't. The truth is that I don't feel well enough to spend a full day in the sun. "That sounds fun. The girls will love it," I say with fake sincerity.

David starts to step off of the porch but hesitates. "Is everything okay, Tess? I mean, I know it's none of my business what you'll be up to tomorrow—what you've been up to, but this secrecy has got me worried."

I try really hard to make my smile not look forced. "Everything is fine, David," I say, knowing full well that everything is most definitely not fine.

"Good," he says. "I'll have the girls home by 8:00."

"Okay," I say. "Have fun." I think about following David to his car so I can say good-bye to the girls once more but then remember that I'm wearing my give-up-on-life sweatpants and an oversized t-shirt, and I don't want to stand anywhere near perfectly-put-together Meredith. Meredith. I wonder why I have such a hard time remembering that. I settle for blowing the girls a kiss. I watch as David backs out of my driveway and wonder if that's how we used to look together back when we were married.

As the car pulls around the corner and out of sight, I turn to go back into my house. It feels empty, not just because I'm the only one home, but because it lacks something every home should have. It's a sort of hollowness, which is so much worse than emptiness.

"You asked for this," I say out loud just to see if my voice echoes. It doesn't.

I really should've made the girls pick up their toys before they left. But then I wouldn't have anything to distract me from thinking about tomorrow. Actually, I'm not nervous about tomorrow, just about finding out the truth about what's wrong with me.

I've told no one about finding the lump last spring, the suspicious mammogram I had a couple months ago, or about the equally dubious ultrasound that followed a couple weeks later. I'd driven myself to the biopsy appointment and was by myself when I received the dreaded phone call informing me that I do indeed have cancer.

The doctor had also found a couple lumps under my arm that he's pretty sure are cancerous as well. Tomorrow I will have a PET scan to see just how much cancer is in me—to see if there is any hope for me to beat this. No matter what the results, I know that I will be alone when I hear my fate, and it's my own fault. David and I may share custody of the girls, but he got custody of our friends.

The only thing that scares me more than living the rest of my life alone is dying alone—being buried alone. I remind myself that my prognosis may not be as dire as I fear. People beat breast cancer every day. Don't they? There's no reason for me to believe that I can't—no reason yet anyway.

I start to feel lightheaded and realize that it's because I'm breathing way too fast. I sit down on the couch and put both hands on my face to try and stop the spinning in my head from my panic. I will my breathing to slow to normal. I curl up on the couch in a fetal position. I'll just rest here a few minutes. I open my eyes hours later to total darkness. I've wasted another day sleeping.

I wonder how the girls are doing, if they miss me, and if someday soon they will wake up in the morning without a mother.

I Am Cancer

CHAPTER TWO

I watch with detachment as the radioactive tracer is injected into my arm. I can't think about why I'm here and what it means to have cancer, but I do. Everything about cancer is terrifying: not knowing how much of my body it has invaded, the treatment, the financial implications of treatment, and possible resulting death from it. In order to live through this, I know that I must endure horrendous physical discomfort, and I'm not sure if I can take it.

But I have to—for my girls.

I turn page after page in a magazine that wouldn't capture my interest even under normal circumstances while I wait for the tracer to move through my body. My brain hops from one terrifying thought to the next in a disoriented manner so rapidly that I can't seem to land on one particular idea. I'm not sure how many times I mindlessly flip through the same magazine before I'm led to the PET Scan room.

"Lie perfectly still," the smiling technician tells me as the table I'm lying on moves into the machine. As the table comes to a stop and the clicking noises of the machine begin, I am overwhelmed with one thought.

David.

There was a time when we were extremely happy together. We met in college on a hiking trip that one of my friends invited me on. Stephanie had a crush on David's friend, Andrew, and wanted me to come along to be her support. I wasn't thrilled to go; I'd never been an outdoorsy type of person, but for Steph, I'd suffer through it.

Steph and I splurged on new hiking boots—Steph had high hopes that this would not be our only opportunity to hike with the guys. I, on the other hand, thought they were cute enough that I wouldn't mind wearing them even if I never hiked again—which I hoped I wouldn't. My biggest mistake, however, was not trying to break them in before the trip. I had blisters on top of my blisters, and before we reached the top of the hill we were climbing, I wondered why in the world anyone would ever think that hiking was fun.

Steph had the motivation to keep pace with Andrew. If her feet were bothering her, I couldn't tell. I, on the other hand, kept falling farther and farther behind the group. I stared at the ground, watching where I would place my next screaming foot. There was only one trail heading up the mountain, so I wasn't worried about getting lost. I concentrated so much on trying not to focus on my throbbing feet that I nearly tripped when David's voice broke through my thoughts.

"New boots?"

He grabbed my arm to keep me from falling. We stood there, staring at each other for a minute before I finally answered him. I realized that I hadn't really looked at him before that moment. His sandy blond hair peeked out from under his baseball cap. The corner of his mouth raised in that crooked smile that would someday become so familiar to me. I'm not sure if it was his touch or that smile that made me catch my breath. There was something special about this man. "Yep," I said.

"We're almost to the top, so we can rest a little before heading back down."

"What do you mean by almost? Your definition might be much different than mine."

He laughed. "It's not too far. I promise." He kept ahold of my elbow as we made our way around the next curve. The top was still not in sight.

"I know this may surprise you, but I don't hike much," I said.

He chuckled and said, "I'd have never guessed."

"Seriously, if it's much farther, I may have to wait here for you guys."

He squeezed my elbow as I stumbled again.

"You can make it; trust me."

I wasn't sure if I believed him. But after about five more switch backs, we'd finally made it. The view was spectacular, even from my seated position.

"Take your boots off," David said as he lowered his backpack to the ground.

"If I do, I'm not sure I'll get 'em back on."

David pulled out a small box filled with Band-Aids and triple antibiotic cream. "Let me see your blisters."

There was something about baring my feet in front of David that made me extremely uncomfortable. "I'll be fine."

He gave me his crooked smile—man, was it appealing—and said, "You really should at least get Band-Aids on them to keep them from rubbing on the way down."

"Give me that," I said, reaching for the box. As I grabbed the box, David smiled wide as he held onto it for a few seconds before letting go. I waited until he was standing with the others before I started unlacing my boots.

I slid my socks off and let the cool breeze ease the stinging of my feet. My heels were the worst, but the outside of my feet also had blisters. When my feet started to get cold, I put the cream and the Band-Aids on. I really didn't want to put my socks and boots back on but walking down the rocky surface barefoot really wasn't an option.

"You should wear thicker socks when you hike."

David's voice startled me. I hadn't realized that he'd been watching, and my face grew hot.

"I'll have to remember that for next time," I said, pretty sure that there wouldn't be a next time.

David rummaged through his bag again and pulled out a pair of thick white socks. "Here, wear these."

"No really, I'll be fine."

"No really," he said, playfully mimicking me, "I insist."

He handed me the socks and held out his hand for me to give him my dirty ones. There was no way that I was going to hand him my sweaty socks. "Thank you," I said, "for the Band-Aids and the socks."

"My pleasure," David said as he stooped to pick up my soiled socks. I snatched them up before he could touch them. He laughed. "Sorry."

When I stood up, I crammed my dirty socks into my pocket. "Are you guys ready?" I said, while thinking, *Let's get this over with.*

The way back down was much easier, although my boots irritated my feet in different areas than climbing had. David was right about the socks. They did help.

To my surprise, when David asked me if I wanted to hike with them again the following week, I said yes. On the ride back to our dorm room, I wondered why in the world I'd agreed, knowing full well the reason.

David.

I grew to love hiking, or maybe it was just that I loved David so much that I told myself that I loved it. I wonder if that's when I started losing myself, when I started being just an extension of David. I don't really know the answer to that because I'm still not sure who I am besides Emmie and Charlotte's mother or David's ex.

When the PET scan is over, something in the technician's eyes as the table comes to a halt tells me that she knows the results, and they aren't good. When I ask her about it, she says that the doctor has to read them and that he will contact me with the results in a few days.

I drink about a gallon of water when I get home, trying to flush the radioactive tracer out of my system. They'd told me that I shouldn't be around pregnant women or small children for at least eight hours after the scan. My girls would be home in nine. I probably should've asked David to keep them overnight again, but he was already suspicious.

David is thirty-three minutes late returning the girls, which usually wouldn't have bothered me. But the stress of the unknown, feeling like crap, and not being able to witness my girls first time at the water park has made me pretty surly. Charlotte had fallen asleep on the way home, so David carries her straight to her bed. While he is tucking her in, Emmie says, "Meredith put way too much sunscreen on me. Dad had to wipe it off with my towel." I can tell that Emmie thinks I'll find humor in Meredith's incompetence, but I don't. I'm furious.

David is smiling when he returns to the living room, which adds to my fury. "Why in the hell was that woman putting sunscreen on *our* daughter?"

At first, David looks simply shocked, but then I see his brown eyes darken and his jaw tighten. "Because I didn't want her to get sunburned."

"Why didn't you do it?"

David stiffens. "I was busy putting sunscreen on Charlotte."

I put my hand on my hip. "Were you not capable of putting it on both of them?"

"What the hell, Tess? Meredith was only trying to help."

"That woman has no business taking care of *our* children. That's your job."

In my frustration, I don't notice that Emmie has begun to cry. David picks her up and holds her close while shooting me a *now look what you've done* look over her shoulder. I should apologize, but I don't. Neither does David.

I reach out and gently take Emmie from David, and she seems to melt into me. I hate myself for picking a fight in front of her. I feel my eyes well up, but I manage to keep from crying in front of David. "Tell your dad good night and thank you for such a fun day."

She raises her head as says, "Bye, Daddy. Thank you."

David rubs her back, kisses her on her forehead, and says, "Bye, baby. I love you."

I realize that David hasn't been this close to me in months. I should take a step back, but all I want to do is lean into him.

"We'll talk about this later," David says as he heads out the door.

I wonder if we will talk about it or if we'll just pretend my little outburst didn't happen. The truth is that I'm not upset with David for letting his girlfriend put sunscreen on our daughter. I'm upset that another woman had stepped into my role as Emmie's mother. Whether or not I live through this cancer of mine, I know that this will not be the last time that it will happen.

I let Emmie sleep in my bed both because I know that I've upset her and because I don't want to be alone.

You asked for this, I tell myself.

CHAPTER THREE

When I wake up, I realize that Charlotte has crawled into bed with Emmie and me. I cuddle with both of them and think about how much I love these girls. I would do anything for them—including apologizing to their dad. My stomach is one huge knot, and I feel terrible for how I acted toward David. I can't believe that was really me.

The girls and I make pancakes together for breakfast and afterwards decide to bake peanut butter chocolate chip cookies—David's favorite. Just as I am pulling the last batch out of the oven, my phone rings. My heart drops when I see that it's my oncologist on the phone.

21

The conversation is short. He has the results of my PET scan and wants me to come to his office tomorrow for him to share them with me. "Make sure you bring someone with you this time," he says. "No one should have to go through this alone."

"I'll try," I say, knowing that I won't.

Mrs. Mills from next door knocks, asking if the girls can come to her house for a few hours to play with her grandkids. The free time allows me to take care of something that I don't want to but know that I need to. I shower, get dressed, and grab a plateful of cookies before making my way to David's office.

As I amble through the office building, I try to remember the last time I visited David here. It was before the divorce—when I was numb. I remember sitting in the chair in front of his desk but not anything we talked about. Those months before we separated are a blur to me. When I try to picture the interactions between David and me back then, it's like looking into a foggy mirror. I see shapes, and I know who was there but nothing else. Only the feeling of being stuck in quicksand and the weight of our failing marriage pushing me under is clear. I step off the elevator on David's floor and immediately spot David's secretary.

"Oh, my goodness, Tess, it's so good to see you," Amy, says as I enter. "How are you, dear?"

I can tell that she is surprised to see me, and I feel ashamed for that. I ignore her question because I can't bring myself to lie to such a sweet lady. She has always treated my girls and me as if seeing us were the best part of her day. "It's good to see you too. You look amazing," I say. "Is he busy?"

She winks at me, smiles, and says, "Why, no, he isn't. Go right in."

"You might want to warn him."

"Nope," she says and gestures me toward his office.

I realize why when I get to his door and hear the voices of Meredith and David. I recognize the tone in his voice—the one that is a mixture of disappointment and frustration—the one that comes just before he loses his temper.

I hated David's temper, not because it was scary, because it wasn't, but because of the way he looked at me when he was angry. The hurt and sadness that came with his irritation with me was hard to look at. Even now I feel the shame at David's tone.

I consider waiting until she leaves to go in but decide, what the hell. I knock on David's open door before stepping in. David's eyes widen upon seeing me. Evidently, he is just as surprised as Amy. "Can I talk to you a minute?"

David doesn't even look toward Meredith when he says, "Can you give us a minute, Mer?"

Meredith's mouth drops open as a squeaking sound escapes from the back of her throat. She crosses her arms and says, "Whatever she has to say to you, she can say it in front of me."

David's jaw tightens; he closes his eyes and lets out a noisy sigh. He glances at her and says, "Please, Meredith. And close the door on your way out."

She looks at me and then back at David as if she was waiting for him to change his mind. She finally accepts defeat and leaves, closing the door firmly behind her.

"I brought a peace offering," I say as I approach David's desk.

He smiles and asks, "Are those?"

I return his smile, a real smile this time, and say, "Peanut butter chocolate chip, yes."

"Thank you."

I plop down in the chair in front of David's desk and say, "I'm really sorry for the way I acted last night."

"It's okay. I understand that it's difficult for another woman to—"

"Yes, it is. It's still no excuse. The divorce was my idea, and I shouldn't be surprised that you're moving on. Having another woman step into my shoes is just part of the deal, right?"

A crease of worry appears on David's forehead. "No one can step into your shoes, Tess. Our girls have one mother. That won't change."

I think about my oncology appointment tomorrow and know that there's a chance that David's words, no matter how well meaning, are probably wrong. I can't expect my girls to grow up motherless, even if the very thought of them calling someone else mom makes me feel sick.

We sit in silence, both lost in our own thoughts. For some reason, my mind goes back to the night our marriage ended. We were sitting in our living room after the kids had gone to bed. We both stared at the television, like we did every night. I can't remember what we were watching or even if I knew at the time. I just remember the heaviness in my chest and the empty feeling in the bottom of my stomach.

There was a time when we took this time to talk, just us, with no interruptions. We used to laugh until our sides hurt and tears ran down our cheeks. It had been years, it seemed, since that happened. We rarely even smiled at each other anymore. For that matter, I rarely smiled at all.

"I think we should get divorced." The words fell from my lips without thought. I don't know what had inspired them. I hadn't been thinking about it, it just happened.

David's eyes widened. He looked at me for a long moment as his dark eyes shifted from shock to hurt and disappointment. I'd come to know that particular expression rather well in those days. I didn't look away like I usually did. I'm not sure how I managed to hold his gaze.

"Are you sure?" He asks in a voice so quiet I almost didn't hear him.

"Yes," I say without looking away.

David stands and starts pacing across the room. He rubs his hands down the front of his pants as if he is trying to wipe something distasteful off of them. He shakes his head over and over, obviously trying to make sense out of what was happening in our living room. "We don't have to rush to this decision. We could go to counseling."

I look out the window. It's as if someone else spoke through my mouth as I said, "I think it's too late for that."

David stops in the middle of the room and I can feel the heat of his gaze on my face. "Okay," he said. Without another word, he turned and left our home.

I stared at the door my husband of fifteen years had disappeared through. I wasn't sad or mad or anything. I was just empty.

I look at David and wonder if he is thinking about the same thing I am. The sadness in his eyes makes me think that the possibility is pretty high that he is.

"Yeah, well, I *am* sorry," I say, apologizing for much more than last night's behavior.

We sit in awkward silence for a few more minutes, both lost in our own regret. "I should go and let you and Meredith get back to whatever you were doing."

As I get up to leave, David says, "Thanks again for the cookies."

I manage a small smile. "You're welcome." I consider asking him to come with me to the doctor's office tomorrow but reject the idea almost immediately. He's not my husband anymore.

I'm almost to the door when David says, "Tess."

I turn to look at him.

"I'm sorry that I didn't fight harder for our family."

My eyes fill with tears. "Me too."

I manage to make it to the car before breaking down. Eighteen months ago, I was sure that I had stopped loving David. Our marriage had gone flat. We'd become more like roommates than a married couple. The girls were the only bonds we had left. Divorce seemed like the only escape from my unhappiness. I didn't realize then that it would only add to it.

Maybe it's facing possible impending death that has awoken my feelings for David. Maybe it was seeing him with Meredith and our daughters pulling out of my driveway a couple days ago. Whatever it is, I know this: I'm still in love with my ex-husband.

How could I have been so stupid?

CHAPTER FOUR

The cancer is everywhere.

I sit in Dr. Sam's office pretending to listen to all he's telling me. In reality, I'm only registering a few words—words like metastasized and stage four. He says something about the cancer being in my liver or kidneys; I can't remember which or whether it's both. It doesn't really matter though because the word that rings the loudest is the one I feared the most: terminal.

"How long?" I manage to say.

Dr. Sam hesitates for a moment. The compassion in his expression almost answers my question. "Three months without treatment—maybe nine with."

Three months. Without treatment, I'll be dead before Christmas.

Could last year really have been my last Christmas? It can't be. I didn't appreciate it enough. I have to have one more Christmas with my girls.

And then I realize that their birthdays are in May. I do a mental count and realize that May is more than nine months away. How could I have experienced the last birthday that my girls will ever have with me without knowing it? It can't be true.

"I need to make it to May," I say. "I'll do whatever it takes to make it until then."

"Why May?"

I swallow hard. I should be crying, but I'm not. This news is too grave for me, and the need to see Emmie turn seven and Charlotte turn four too great for me to give in to weakness. "My girls' birthdays."

"Well," Dr. Sam says, "I can't guarantee that you will make it that long, but I will give it my best shot."

"As will I," I say.

Dr. Sam takes nearly thirty more minutes to explain my treatment plan. His words are filled with terrifying images of severe side effects that I will experience from the chemo. Extreme fatigue and nausea mark the top of the list.

"Will I lose my hair?"

"I'm afraid so." Dr. Sam says.

It's just one more item on the long list of things that cancer will take from me. I've had long hair nearly my whole life, and I can't imagine running my fingers through it and pulling it out in clumps. I can't think about any of it, but I do.

"Do you have any more questions?"

I shake my head. Actually, I have many questions, but I'm not sure that I want the answers to them, so I don't ask. The answers don't matter anyway. I'll do whatever it takes to make it until May.

On the way home I stop at a walk-in hair salon and have all of my hair cut off. It's pixie short, and for the first time ever, I realize that my ears stick out. My eyes fill with tears as I look at my own reflection. I look completely different without my long hair, which is totally appropriate because I *am* a completely different person than I was before I walked into my oncologist's office.

I'm not just someone living with cancer; I'm dying of it.

I pick up pizza on my way home and barely make it there before David arrives with the girls.

"You cut your hair," David says, and I know he doesn't like it any more than I do. He always loved my long hair.

I smile and wonder if he can tell that it's a fake one. I run my fingers through what hair I have left and say, "I just needed a change."

"Well, it's definitely different," he says. "It looks good."

I know he's lying, but that's fine because I appreciate the fact that he's trying not to hurt my feelings.

"Do you want a slice of pizza?" I ask.

David smiles his crooked smile and says, "I wish I could, but I have dinner plans."

Meredith. Pretty young-looking Meredith. Meredith with the long hair. Meredith who doesn't have cancer and will live much longer than nine months. Meredith who will be around to mother my children after I am gone.

I hate Meredith.

"Would it be possible for you to keep the girls on Fridays for a couple of months? I have something that I need to take care of."

David's eyes narrow. "Yeah. I can work that out."

"Great. Thanks," I say still smiling. My cheeks start to hurt from the effort. David is staring at my head, and I feel my face heat up.

I'm definitely getting a hat to wear. One that will hide this haircut as well as my bald head.

"Well, I better go."

"Okay."

"This Friday then?" he asks.

"If it's not too much trouble."

"It's no trouble," David says as he turns to leave. He hesitates by the door. "Is everything okay, Tess?"

I almost tell him the truth. "Everything is fine," I say. I can see the creases in David's forehead and know that he is trying to decide if I'm telling him the truth. He shakes his head and steps out the door.

Friday is my first of six chemo treatments. It's the first day of my fight to throw my girls one last birthday party.

I have to make it to May.

CHAPTER FIVE

The first two chemo treatments were difficult, but this third one is excruciating. I've already lost all of my hair and had somehow managed to keep it from David. I started to wear a baseball cap right after I cut my hair off. When I had hair, it was so short, it barely showed beneath my cap, so I don't look much different now that I'm bald. I just draw my eyebrows on every day and try to give myself a little color with makeup. It's been good enough to fool the girls, but I'm sure that if David saw me up close, he'd notice. Last week, I'd watched for him from the window and sent the girls out to his car when he pulled in. This morning, I'd wrapped a towel around my head and waved from the front door as the girls met David outside again. If David is suspicious about my strange behavior, he doesn't let on.

The nausea this time hits me hard. I'm too weak to keep running to the bathroom, so I bring a pillow and blanket and sleep on the bathroom floor. By the time I realize that the girls are home, it's too late to put myself back together. I force myself to a sitting position, which immediately triggers vertigo. I slam my eyes closed and lean my head against the wall to stop the spinning in my head. Emmie finds me in the bathroom and immediately starts screaming.

"It's alright, Emmie," I say as I hold my drooping arms out for her. I still can't lift my head from the wall. David appears in the doorway, holding Charlotte.

"Jesus, Tess," he says. The horror in his eyes expresses magnitudes. There's no hiding my cancer now.

David pulls out his cell phone and speaks quickly into it. "You go on without me. Something's come up." "Take my car, I'll get myself home."

I've got to get out of this bathroom. I kiss Emmie on the forehead and say, "Let me up, Baby." Before she moves, I hear the front door slam.

"What are you doing in here?" David says. He looks down the hall and then notices me trying to get up. "Tess, wait," he says firmly as he sets Charlotte down and steps out of sight. Charlotte climbs on my lap next to Emmie. I stay put, which is totally out of character for me. I shouldn't eaves drop, but I can't help it. I don't have to try too hard because David's shouting.

"I said something's come up."

"What will I tell Phillip and Pam?"

"Tell them I had an emergency."

"What emergency?" Meredith's voice seems closer.

"Not your concern." David says.

"We've been planning this for weeks," Meredith screeches.

"Leave, Meredith." David's firm voice leaves no room for negotiation. "Now!"

The door slams, and David returns. "Okay, girls let's get your mom to bed." I'm not sure how his tone changed from furious to calm so quickly. I know it's an act he's putting on for the girls because I'm sure he's just as pissed at me as he is Meredith. David supports my weight as I shuffle to my bed. I glance in the mirror as I walk past. I'm pale as a fish that has lain dead in the sun for days, and I wish so much that David wouldn't have seen me like this. He's gentle as he helps me into what used to be our bed.

I wake up some time later to find David sitting on the bed next to me. His head rests on the headboard, his eyes closed. I watch him for a while before getting up to use the restroom. David's eyes are open when I return. I crawl back into bed and say, "So, I have cancer."

"No shit," He says. "Why in the hell didn't you tell me?"

My mind goes blank. I'd envisioned this moment so many times. I'd thought that I'd considered every possible scenario, but I hadn't dreamed it would be anything like this, lying in bed, bald and weak as a newborn kitten. I should have grabbed my baseball cap on my way back to bed. I'm more vulnerable in this moment than I've ever been.

"It's not your problem anymore."

"What the hell is that supposed to mean," David snaps. "You're the mother of my children, of course it's my problem." His eyes bore into me, not in a mean way, but in a way that makes me realize that he still cares about me, not only because I'm the mother of his children, but because I'm me, whoever that is.

I'm so ashamed. Again. I seem to have screwed everything up when it comes to David. "I'm sorry. I should have told you."

"Damn right you should have," he says and then in a softer tone, "Is it breast cancer?"

"Yes. Stage 4. It's in both breasts, lymph nodes, liver, one lung, hell, it's everywhere. I'm basically more cancer now than I am me."

David rubs his forehead. "You can fight this. People beat cancer every day."

"People may," I say, "but not me."

"Damn it, Tess, of course you can. You have to."

I want to tell him that I have a chance just to keep him from knowing the truth, but I can't lie anymore about this. "I'm dying, David." It's the first time that I've said the words out loud, and somehow, I accept it.

"Then why go through this?" He says, waving his hands toward me.

"The doctor told me I have three months without treatment, maybe nine with."

"Unless the treatment kills you first."

Of all of the people in the world, David is the only one who would understand what I say next. "I have to make it until May."

David stays quiet for a while, looking past me. Tears fall rapidly down his cheeks as reality sets in. "Does your mom know?"

"God, no. Why would I tell her?"

"Because she's your mother."

"What am I supposed to tell her, David? 'I know I've only spoken to you twice in the last fifteen years, but I thought I should let you know that I'm dying.'"

I realize that David has scooted closer to me. He takes my hand and says, "She has a right to know. Wouldn't you want to know if it were Emmie or Charlotte?"

Outraged, I say, "I would never let that much time go by without speaking to my daughters." And then it hits me. I will go a lifetime without speaking to my daughters. Their lifetimes. For the first time since Dr. Sam gave me my prognosis, I cry.

David lies down next to me and pulls me into his arms, and I sob on his shoulder until we eventually fall asleep. We're still in this position when I hear one of the girls in the bathroom.

It's time to start another day, one of the few I have left. I wish that I could stop time and stay in this moment, so I don't have to go through any more chemo, and the cancer doesn't get any closer to killing me. I just want to lie in David's arms and listen to my girls in the other room.

But time never stands still.

CHAPTER SIX

I don't want to get out of bed. I've finally
started to feel like I can function, although
barely, and my fourth chemo treatment is in a
couple hours. I hope I won't be as sick as I was
last time but know that I probably will be. I stare
at the ceiling and notice cobwebs in the corner.
I'll have to get the broom later.

I've lain here too long. David will be here
to pick up the girls soon, so I have to get moving.
At least I don't have to worry about fixing my
hair, so getting ready won't take too long. I sit on
the side of my bed, knowing that the first steps of
the day are going to be painful. I feel ninety-four.
My bones ache, and my head feels heavy. How

45

can chemo make me exhausted and at the same time give me insomnia? At least after today I'll be over halfway through my chemo.

David arrives just as I'm finished cleaning up after breakfast. Instead of picking up the girls, he brings a babysitter, so he can take me to my appointment.

"It'll be so boring, David. You don't have to come with me."

He gives me his crooked smile. "I'm not going to let you go through any more of this alone, Tess," he says. "And don't give me any crap about how you aren't my concern anymore because that's just stupid."

"David," I say and then tears pour down my face. I can't find words to express my relief. I hadn't realized how heavy the burden of getting myself to and from these appointments was until it was lifted by my ex-husband. I turn to get my shoes from the bedroom. I'm shocked, confused, and so very grateful.

The chemo itself isn't terribly painful as it's administered—just a little burning. Most of the discomfort is mental. The dread of what I will feel like in a few hours is definitely the worst.

David sits in a chair next to me reading a magazine. We haven't spoken much since we left my house. I was too filled with dread on the drive over. David seems overwhelmed with everything as well. This is one place that we can't ignore my illness. Cancer isn't just inside of me; it's a physical presence that sits between me and the rest of the world. It's a constant reminder that by this time next year, I will be dead, and I'm terrified.

"Do you believe in heaven?" I ask David.

"Of course," he says with wide eyes. He closes his magazine and sets it on the table beside him. "Don't you?"

"I always have," I say, "only now that death is so close, I'm afraid that—" I close my eyes, trying to think of words to describe my

47

fear. My ears pulse with my pounding heartbeat and my breathing speeds up. Every time I imagine what it will be like when I'm gone, imagine what I'll be doing in heaven, I can't get beyond the fear of the unknown. Could I possibly be afraid of heaven? No, that's not it. It's much worse than fearing heaven. I open my eyes to find David has moved closer to me. "What if I just stop existing, David? What if I close my eyes and then nothing? Tess Peterson just…stops? Then what would be the point?"

"The point of what?"

I swallow hard. "Of me."

David rubs his face and then runs his hands through his hair. "Jesus, Tess. What's the point of you? Do you think that just because you're dying your life doesn't have purpose? Without you, there would be no Emmie or Charlotte. Hell, without you, I can't imagine what my life would be like." His voice cracks, and his eyes well up. He grabs my hand. "I have no idea how any of us will go on without you."

David uses his free hand to wipe his face. "How am I possibly supposed to raise the girls without their mother?" Shaking his head, he says, "I have to believe in heaven, Tess, because I just can't imagine a world without you existing."

"I'm scared, David."

"So am I."

We sit in silence, both staring at nothing. I wonder what David and the girls will be doing a year from now. What will I be doing?

Will I be?

I Am Cancer

CHAPTER SEVEN

This week's chemo hasn't hit me as hard
as last week's. David had stayed over on Friday
night, sleeping on the couch, just in case I needed
help. I didn't. The drugs that they gave me to
counteract my nausea worked better this time. He
kept the girls Saturday and Sunday even though
it wasn't his weekend to have them. By
Wednesday, I've regained enough energy to bake
cookies for the girl's after-school snack. We're
sitting at the kitchen table finishing up when
David arrives to pick up the girls.

"You look good," David says.

I know I don't really look good. I'm pale
with dark circles under my eyes. Even with my

hat on, my baldness is obvious. I wear it mostly to keep my head warm now that the truth is out about my cancer. Looking good is relative. I look good compared to how I looked over the weekend. "I don't feel too bad," I say.

David's smile reaches his eyes this time, and I realize that I hadn't seen him smile like this in a long time. "Do you feel well enough to come with us tonight? We're going out for pizza and then to mini-golf course after dinner."

"How will Meredith feel about that?" The words are out of my mouth before I can consider the wisdom of them.

"Not relevant."

"Daddy and Meredith broke up," Emmie says.

I look at David. He shrugs. I'm not sure what to say. Should I tell him I'm sorry even though I'm not. This news makes me happy— makes me hopeful somehow. "I'd love to come. But I don't know how much competition I'll be in my frail condition." I say smiling.

"Already coming up with excuses?" David asks. His crooked smile is even more attractive on him now that I know that Meredith is no longer on the receiving end of it. After the girls leave to get their shoes, David says, "Don't think that I'm going to take it easy on you just because you're dying."

"I would expect nothing different."

I can only eat a half a slice of pizza and by the fourth hole of mini-golf, I'm so tired that I can barely manage to drag my club. I sit on a bench to watch David and the girls take their turns. As I watch David patiently help our daughters line up their shots and encouraging them when they miss the hole, I am amazed at his patience. He has always been incredibly patient, even when I had given him every reason not to be. Maybe that's why he accepted my desire for a divorce so easily. I'd thought that he left that night because he wanted to end our marriage as much as I did. Now, I'm not so sure.

Why had he asked me to come tonight? Was it pity for his dying ex-wife or was it because he wanted to be with *me*? Now that Meredith is out of the picture, I'm not sure what his motivation is.

"Mom, it's your turn." Emmie says.

"Let your mom rest for a bit. She can watch you from there," David says.

Every joint and muscle in my body screams at me to stay put, but my heart wants to join in the fun with my little family. When I stand, I wonder if anyone can hear the creaking of my body. "I'm no quitter, David Peterson. You are going down."

David's grin almost makes all my pain go away. We play nine holes instead of eighteen. David makes an excuse that since it's a school night, the girls needed to get home and to bed, but I know it's because he knows how exhausted I am.

We eat cookies dipped in milk for a bedtime snack before David tucks the girls in for the night. I'm just finishing wiping off the table when he comes back to the kitchen.

"I should be tucking you into bed as well by the way you look," he says.

"Thanks?" I say, leaning hard on the edge of the counter.

David chuckles. "Seriously, you need to get some rest."

I really do need rest. I need my strength to tackle chemo number five. "Thank you for inviting me along tonight."

David walks across the room and stands in front of me. "Thank you for coming," he says as he steps so close that we're almost touching. We stare at each other for a few moments before he does the unexpected. He kisses me. Not just a quick peck on the cheek, he really kisses me, and for a moment we are David and Tess again.

God, I've missed this.

"Now, do I need to tuck you in, or can I trust you to go to bed right after I leave?"

My legs feel weak, and I wonder if I will have to crawl to bed. For now, the counter is holding me up. I don't want David to know how frail I am. "I can get myself to bed."

David takes my ball cap off and rubs my head. "I've been dying to do that."

"Smooth as a baby's butt," I say.

David starts for the door and turns back. "Good night, Tess. I'll pick you up on Friday morning."

"David, you don't have to—"

He puts his hand up in a stop motion. "I'm going with you to your chemo appointment. I told you that you aren't going through this alone anymore."

"Thank you," I say, not even trying to hide my relief.

The front door closes, and I close my eyes, replaying what just happened in my kitchen. Wouldn't it be something if we finally figured out how to be happy together just in time for me to die?

CHAPTER EIGHT

Life for the last couple weeks fell into a kind of rhythm. David took me to my chemo appointments, spent the night on the couch on Friday nights, and kept the girls on the weekends. He came by every weeknight as well to check up on us. This morning, as I sit with the girls in the kitchen and wait for him to take me to my final chemo appointment, I can't help but wonder how things will change once I'm no longer recovering from being poisoned. I'm not sure how I'll feel physically when all of this is over. I'll still be dying after all. I hope that I'll feel good enough for a while to make some more memories with my girls. My breath catches at this thought.

Memories for whom? My girls are so young. I was about Emmie's age when my grandmother died, and I have very few, very fuzzy memories of her. What if, in a few years, that's all I become to my daughters—a fuzzy memory? Will they know how much I love them? Will they know what I put myself through in order to gain a few more months with them? Why am I working so hard to gain just a few months? It's not like it will make much difference to Emmie and Charlotte—unless I make it to May. I have to make it to May.

"Why are you sad, Mommy," Charlotte says. I hadn't realized that I'd started crying.

"I'm not sad, sweetie," I lied. And then I speak the truest words that I've ever spoken. "I'm just thinking about how much I love you and your sister."

"So, these are happy tears?" Emmie says.

I nod and gather both girls into my lap, holding them tight. I cry into their hair and they both pat me on the back.

When I open my eyes, David is there watching us.

"Girls, look. Daddy's here," I say. They slide from my lap and run to their father. I pad silently to the bathroom to wash my face. "Stop crying," I tell myself. I don't want the girls to see me crying like this. I don't want them to know how terribly sad I am right now. I don't want them to remember me this way—bald and weak and bawling. I want them to remember me smiling and laughing—to remember how much fun we had together as a family.

The tears won't stop. I splash and splash cold water on my face but can't seem to pull myself together. David taps on the door, and I let him in. He doesn't say anything, just puts his arms around me and cries with me. I cling to him as if he's my lifeline, as if he's still mine, and I ask myself, "Am I still his?"

I'm not sure which one of us lets go first. We stand side by side in front of my bathroom mirror, blowing and wiping and splashing. "So," David says, "why are we crying?"

And I laugh. At first, it's a hysterical, crazy kind of laugh, but then it turns into a genuine, from the gut laugh. It's just so absurd. Minutes before, I couldn't stop crying and now I can't stop laughing. I'm dying, very soon, but not before I experience excruciating pain and lose all my strength, and my girls may not remember me. And David will probably find someone else to marry. And my girls will have a new mother to make precious memories with—a new mother who will be there for all their milestones. A new mother to sit with David as Emmie and Charlotte graduate high school or college. A new mother to watch David walk them down the aisle—to be with them when they give birth to my grandchildren. I'm scared, so very terrified of what is happening to my body and what will happen to my girls when I'm gone.

And I can't stop laughing. I'm sure David thinks that my sanity is slipping, and he's probably right.

"Do you have any idea what it's like to know you don't have a future beyond the next few months—to finally start getting your shit together only to die before you can fix all of the things you've screwed up in your life? And, damn it, I'm crying again"

David wipes the tears from my face and holds me again. He kisses my bald head and murmurs, "I'm so sorry, Tess." He doesn't tell me that everything will be okay, which I appreciate because everything will not be okay.

Somehow, I manage to stop crying. I wash my face and say, "Let's get this over with."

"You don't have to go to this last chemo appointment if you don't want to." His brown eyes are soft as he holds my gaze, and I realize that it really would be okay if I chose not to have this last treatment. It probably wouldn't make much of a difference in my life span. But I won't quit. Not this time.

"I'm ready now," I say, and I mean it. My goal is to make it to May, and if going through one more chemo treatment will help me do that, then I'm going to do it, no matter how much I dread it.

David holds out his hand to me and I take it. The girls are outside playing with Pam, so they hardly notice when we tell them goodbye out the back door.

The car is stuffy. It's hard to breathe in the cramped space. I try cracking my window, but it doesn't seem to help. I roll it back up and realize why I'm so uncomfortable. It's too quiet in here. Eerily quiet—as if David and I were afraid to make any noise—to even take a deep breath. I open the window again to block out the silence. I lean my head against the headrest and close my eyes.

"I know I can't possibly understand what it's like for you to—" David's words drop off.

"Be dying?" I ask.

David nods.

"There's just not enough time left, David. There are so many things I want to do with the girls, so many things that I want to say to them. I want to make precious memories with them in the little time I have left, but what for? They're so little; they won't remember anything I manage to do with them before I get too sick."

"Is that it?" David says. "You're afraid Emmie and Charlotte won't remember you?"

I can't answer. I swallow hard but still can't speak from the lump in my throat.

"Don't be stupid, Tess. Of course, they'll remember you!"

"But I was Emmie's age when my grandmother died, and no matter how hard I try, I can't remember her," I rasp. "I remember feeling safe and loved around her, but I can't remember anything we did together. I can't even remember what she looked like. I don't even have a photo of her."

"They won't forget you, Tess. I won't let them. We're going to spend the next few months having fun with our girls. We'll take hundreds of photos, so even if it were possible for them to forget what you look like, they won't have to." David pulls into the hospital parking lot and, by some miracle, finds a spot right away. He shuts off the car and turns his deep brown eyes to me. "And you—you can write down everything you want to say to them, and I will make sure they read your words when they are old enough."

The intensity in his stare is so great that I have to look away.

"Tess," he says firmly. "Tess, look at me." He gently grabs my chin and turns my face toward him. "You will not stop existing when you die. Even after you've gone to heaven, you will live on here in our girls. You will live on in me."

"Okay," I say. "Thank you, David."

CHAPTER NINE

I know we should get out of the car, but
for some reason, we just sit there staring out the
windshield. David gets out first and comes
around to the passenger side and opens my door.
I take his offered hand and he helps me out. We
take a couple of steps toward the hospital and
then David pulls me in his arms again. Only this
time is different. This time, he is not just
comforting me. This time, he pulls me tight
against him until there is no space between us. I
lay my head on his chest, knocking my hat off.
The sun is hot on my head.

I feel David's heartbeat against my cheek.
It's been so long since he's held me like this that

65

it feels both foreign and familiar at the same time. It's as if we are two pieces of a puzzle that fit perfectly together, and I wish with all my heart that it wouldn't have to end.

David kisses the top of my bald head gently. I tighten my grip on my ex-husband and say, "I love you, David," and we both hold our breaths.

David clears his throat. "I love you too, Tess. Always have. Always will." His voice is husky and soft.

Too soon, David loosens his hold on me, and we turn toward the hospital. He keeps his arm across my shoulder as we make our way toward the first last time that we will experience in the upcoming months. I can't help but wonder how often I will see him after today.

David holds my hand as the poison is administered. His brows are tightly knit with concern. For the first time, I understand that my part in this, my dying, is the easy part. In a few months, this whole ordeal will be over for me, but it won't be over for David. It won't be over for Emmie and Charlotte. Cancer is not only stealing my life it's also altering the lives of everyone I love. It is not just a disease that will obliterate me, it will also shatter my family.

I hate cancer.

David squeezes my hand, pulling me out of my melancholy. "Tess, I've been thinking." The corner of his mouth turns up. God, I love being on the receiving end of that again. He reaches over to grab my other hand and moves in front of me. "We should get married again."

"What?"

"I mean it. We need to get married again."

My heart is racing. I'm afraid that David is just deciding this in the heat of the moment. We've had an incredibly emotional morning. I'm even more terrified that he'll change his mind once he's had time to really think about what he's saying.

"Are you sure?"

"Absolutely." His smile is wide now, and his brown eyes have a sparkle to them that I haven't seen in far too long.

"Why?"

David's mouth drops open. "What do you mean, why?" He sits on the edge of my chair, facing me.

I know I should answer, but I just can't.

"You love me, right?"

"Yes," I whisper.

"And, I love you, Tess, more than you know."

"But the divorce—it was my fault. I didn't think you'd ever want to—after how I destroyed our family." Hot tears roll down my face.

"Damn it, Tess. Stop it." David looks away and I know that I've ruined the moment. "Stop taking all of the blame. You may have said the words, but I left that night. I left you and our girls without even questioning you. Without fighting." He shakes his head and squeezes his eyes shut. When he opens them, his expression is gentle. "I regretted leaving almost immediately. I sat at the corner stop sign for several minutes, trying to convince myself to turn around and go back. But my pride wouldn't let me.

"I knew you'd been unhappy, and I thought that I couldn't make you happy even if I tried. The problem is that I didn't try very hard. In fact, I didn't try at all. You said the words, but I'm the one that failed."

"David—"

"No, let me finish. I want to marry you again to right the worst wrong I've ever committed. I want our girls to see us together for the rest of your life. I want to be able to show them how much I love their mother and that they should never settle for less than that. Let's mend our broken family. What do you say, Tess? Will you marry me?"

I swallow hard, trying to dislodge the lump in my throat. "Can we get married in a church this time?"

"I don't care where we do it."

"Okay," I say.

David leans in and kisses me, and for the first time in weeks, I'm not thinking about dying.

CHAPTER TEN

David and I got married at the courthouse the first time around. Neither of us had family that we'd wanted to invite. We couldn't justify the money that a large wedding would require. We asked our two closest friends, Steph and Andrew, to be our witnesses. I wore a ten-dollar white sundress that I'd found on a clearance rack at JCPenney, and David wore the one and only suit he'd owned at the time. It wasn't the fairytale wedding that most girls dream of, but at the end of the day, we were just as married after ten minutes with a judge as we would've been had we been married at our church. We thought at the time that we would renew our vows in a church one day, but that had never happened.

This time, I want a proper wedding in a church. I don't need anything fancy or elaborate, I don't have time for that, just a simple ceremony with a few close friends and our daughters as flower girls. I run my fingers down my new white dress and dream about our wedding that will take place this Saturday. I can't believe how excited I am to be David's wife, even more this time around because I know what it's like to live without him.

"Tess," David calls from the living room. He'd been running errands with the girls for a few hours.

"In the bedroom," I say.

When I see the expression on David's face as he enters our bedroom, my stomach drops. "Don't kill me, okay?"

"What did you do?"

David puts his hands on my shoulders and guides me to the bed. "You need to sit down for this."

Oh, God.

"I ran into your mother. I promise, Tess that I didn't contact her. It was just a chance meeting, but perhaps it was providential."

My stomach feels as if it has morphed into a metal ball—a spinning metal ball. "You didn't invite her to the wedding did you?"

He looks up as if he is contemplating how to answer the question.

"David."

"Well, no. I didn't exactly invite her to the wedding. The girls did."

"What?!"

He pats my shoulders a couple times. "Wait, Tess. I need to tell you something."

"Go on."

"Well, when she asked about you, Emmie let it slip that you're bald now, which, of course—she deduced that you are sick."

I put both hands on my face and rub my aching head.

"You know that I wanted you to tell your mother about the cancer, and I don't want you to believe that I went behind your back and told her because I didn't." David kneels down in front of me and gently removed my hands from my face. "I wouldn't do that. You know that, don't you?"

I nod.

"But…I didn't know what to do. The girls were there, and she wanted so badly to see you." He grips both of my hands, in order to ground me, I think. Dread wraps itself around me as I brace for the next words. "She's here, Tess."

"What?!" I pull my hands free and put them on my head. I never missed having hair this much before if only so I could rip it out. "Why did you bring her here, David?" I stand and start pacing the room. "To our home?"

"I'm sorry, Tess, if I handled this all wrong. But she's here now, and maybe it will be good for you to talk to her."

"For closure?" I snap. "There are a lot of things that I should confront before I die, David, but talking to my mother is not one I'd considered. I closed the door to a relationship with her a long time ago."

David steps in front of me to stop my pacing and pulls me into his arms. "I know, and I'm so sorry." He kisses my head. "You don't have to have a relationship with her, but I think you should at least talk to her."

The last person in the world I want to talk to is my mother. I'd avoided seeing her for over fifteen years—since she chose that loser of a husband over me. My actual father left us when I was six. I don't remember him at all, and I have no idea what happened to him after that. I tell myself that I don't care where he is, but that's just a lie. Knowing that my own father abandoned me without ever trying to contact me is a burden that I've carried most of my life—a burden I'm sure to bring to my grave.

The rest of my childhood consisted of accepting men into our home whom my mother hoped would stop her loneliness and help carry the burden of single parenthood. The problem with that mentality is that none of these men were my father, and none of them had any desire to pretend to be.

Of all the men my mother welcomed into our house, only one married her: Frank Watson. Frank was a drunk, a poor provider, and a moocher. I was a teenager when they met, and I knew what he was from the start. My mother did not, or at least she pretended not to. Frank and I hated each other, and if there were a side to take in an argument between the man and me, my mother always chose his. So, the day I turned eighteen, I left my mother's home and never looked back.

I've talked to my mother exactly twice since then: once to tell her that I was married and once to tell her about the birth of Emmie. I sent her pictures of David and me and some of

Emmie, but my mother never even responded. I didn't bother informing her about Charlotte. And now, after all this time of her having absolutely no interest in my wellbeing, she is at my home, waiting to speak to me. Every part of me screams to refuse to see her, but I know that I have to.

"Where is she?"

"Out front with the girls."

"You left our daughters alone with her?!"

David runs his fingers through his hair and says, "I didn't know what else to do. I had to warn you before she came in."

I nod, grab my hat, and head for the kitchen. I'm sitting at the table when David returns with my mother, Emmie and Charlotte each holding one of her hands. I want to tell them to get away from that woman. Instead, I say, "Did you girls have fun with your dad?"

"Yes!" Emmie says, "and we found Grandma."

I shoot a look at David. He smiles apologetically. He stands behind my chair and places his hands on my shoulders.

"Hello, Tess," my mother says.

"Hello," I say as my gaze brushes past her. Looking at her is impossible at this moment.

"Well," David says. "The girls and I will get out of your way."

"I grab David's hand and pull, forcing him to lean his face next to mine. "Don't leave me with her," I whisper.

"Let me take the girls next door, and I'll be right back." He leans in and kisses me on the lips. "Girls, let's go see if Mrs. Mills is home."

My mother walks over to the table and puts her hands on the back of the chair opposite me. I nod, letting her know it's okay for her to sit down.

"Is it breast cancer?" she asks.

"It started as breast cancer, and now it's spread." I don't tell her that I'm dying.

My mother shakes her head. "There's nothing harder than fighting cancer. I was lucky to have caught mine early."

My breath catches in my throat, and I am incapable of responding. All I can do is stare at her. David is just coming through the front door as my voice returns to me. "You had breast cancer, and you didn't tell me?!" I know I sound hysterical, but I don't care.

"I didn't want to worry you." My mother has the audacity to sound confused by how upset I am.

"When?" I ask, narrowing my eyes. "When was this, *Mother*?" I know that she has always hated it when I called her mother instead of mom. It could be because it was always a way for me to distance myself from her. Right now, I want her as far away from me as possible.

"I've been cancer free for ten and a half years now," she says, obviously proud of herself.

I have a difficult time catching my breath. I look at David, who has made it to the kitchen doorway, and give him a look that says *help me*. David moves to stand behind me again with his hands on my shoulders. It's as if I suck some of David's strength through the connection.

"Ten years," I say. My voice is calmer than I feel. "You had breast cancer, a genetically-passed disease, ten years ago, and you didn't think it was important to inform me?"

My mother stammers before saying, "Like I said, I didn't want to worry you."

Her words sound selfless, but I know better. She just didn't want me to see her in a weakened state—like she is seeing me now. The difference is that I will never be able to look back on my weakened state with pride for having survived it.

"I'm dying, Mother," I say. "My cancer is terminal because I wasn't lucky like you. By the time I was diagnosed, it was too late for me." I lean forward, making sure she feels my next words. "Had I known that my own mother had breast cancer, I would've known to get checked for it. I could have beaten cancer, like you, had I known. I wouldn't be trying to cram a lifetime of experiences with my daughters into the few months that I have left." The next words I say slowly. "I'm dying because of you."

I can see that I have hurt her, just as I'd intended. But it doesn't make me feel better having hurt her like I thought it would. All these years, I knew that she had no clue how deeply that she had hurt me. I longed for her to feel what I had. Well, I've finally done it. But instead of feeling justified, I feel terrible.

"You're dying?" she whispers. "But I thought…" She covers her face with her hands and weeps.

I don't cry though. It's as if I'm watching this exchange between my mother and me instead of participating in it. David squeezes my shoulders and says, "Tess."

I can't take it. I can't sit here and watch my mother fall apart, and I can't make myself comfort her. She needs to understand what she

81

has done. "I need to use the bathroom," I say and leave the room.

I'm not sure how long I sit on the edge of the tub. My back aches, and my legs have fallen asleep. I stand up and look in the mirror. I don't want to be the bitter, cruel person that I'd been in the kitchen with my mother. I know that I need to apologize for my behavior. Part of me is afraid that if I apologize to her, it will release from her the responsibility for all that she has done. But maybe it's time to release her from that too. I could put it off and give her time to let my mean words really sink in, but I don't have that kind of time. Do I really want to leave this world, having caused my mother so much misery?

No. No, I don't—even if she deserves some of it.

I open the door to the bathroom and hear David's deep voice. His calming voice chases the rest of my fury away. As I return to the kitchen, I say, "I'm sorry, Mom. I should never had said those things." I grab three glasses from the cupboard. "Would you like something to drink? Water, lemonade?"

"Water would be great," she says, and I can hear the relief in her voice.

I set three glasses of ice water on the table and sit next to David. The table separating my mother and me provides me with a little comfort. I'm not ready for all of the walls between us to fall. We talk about superficial subjects at first. She tells me what she's been doing the years we were apart, and I force myself to let her into a little of my life. She tells me that Frank has mellowed over the years and that he's been sober for over ten years. He'd quit drinking when she was diagnosed with cancer because she needed him to take care of her instead of the other way around. "You'd like him now, I think," she says, but I doubt that.

We don't talk about the divorce or the reason David and I are remarrying. We don't broach the topic of my father's whereabouts, but I still hope I'll be able to have answers to that before I die. I know I'll need to speak to my mother about that sometime, but we've endured enough emotional topics for today.

My mother tells me that she won't come to the wedding if I don't want her to, but I tell her that the girls would be disappointed if their grandmother didn't get to see them doing their flower-girl duties. She could even bring Frank if she wanted, but she said that she would come alone if she chose to come.

I walk my mother to the door, and just before she leaves, she says, "I'm so sorry Tess. For everything." She gives me a quick hug and leaves.

As I turn around, David is leaning against the wall with his arms crossed and his crooked smile on his face. I walk right into his arms, and as he holds me, he says, "I'm so proud of you."

I love this man more now than I ever have. I can't believe that he brought my mother to our home two days before our wedding, but I'm not angry about it anymore. Maybe it was divine providence that made David and my mother cross paths today. He was right. I needed closure.

David goes next door to get the girls while I finish cleaning up the kitchen. I'm exhausted from all of the intense emotions from today, but my fatigue goes much deeper. I can't help thinking about the scan that I will have tomorrow. David is hopeful that the chemo that I endured will have reduced my tumors. But I know that it hasn't. I know that I'm no better, but I can't tell him that. He needs this wedding weekend to be filled with hope. He needs this weekend to be a celebration of our little family. We both do.

I Am Cancer

CHAPTER ELEVEN

"I can't do it, David. I can't wear a wig. It's scratchy and looks as if I have some type of roadkill on top of my head."

David laughs. He steps behind me looking in the mirror at my reflection. He snatches the wig off of my head and says, "Good. I like you better this way."

I know it's supposed to be bad luck for the bride and groom to see each other before the wedding, but really, how much more bad luck could two people have? "But I don't want to be bald for our wedding," I say. "I can't handle the way people look at me and my bald head. All they see is my cancer. I *am* cancer in their eyes, not me."

"But you're not bald anymore," he says as he rubs the fuzz on my head.

"I don't even have eyebrows."

David slides his arms around my waist and puts his chin on my shoulder, still looking in the mirror. "Can't you draw those on?"

I sigh. "Yes, but I can't draw more hair on my head."

He smiles wide and kisses my neck. "Wait here. I have a surprise for you."

He returns to the bathroom carrying a white gift bag with light blue tissue paper sticking out of it. "I thought this might be an issue today, so I got you something."

I pull the tissue paper out of the bag and look in. I laugh. David reaches in and pulls out a white laced ball cap and puts it on my head. "Perfect," he says.

I turn toward the mirror. "It *is* perfect," I say. "Thank you."

David turns me toward him and leans in to give me a kiss but is stopped by the bill of the hat. He rubs his forehead and says, "You finish getting ready while I check on the girls."

Emmie and Charlotte perform their flower-girl duties with enthusiasm, looking adorable in their pale blue dresses. When we were deciding on the color they would wear, they both wanted to wear pink. But I just couldn't bring myself to have a Breast Cancer Awareness wedding. As David walks me down the aisle, I have to remind myself that this is not a dream. I look around at our small group of friends and notice that sitting in a pew by herself is my mother. I had thought that I didn't want her to show up; but seeing her there makes me realize that I secretly did.

I barely remember saying our vows at our first wedding, but this time, I savor each word. This time, I truly understand what it means to love and honor someone, what it means to stick around through terrible illness, and what it means to say that we will be together until death—until death snatches me away from our little family. This time, our vows are more than just words to say in order to get married. This time, saying our vows is more like exchanging pieces of ourselves—as if we are actually becoming one. It's funny how it took losing our marriage to really understand the value of the promises that we now make to each other in front of God, our children, and our friends.

We are both emotional as we exchange rings, and when it was time for the kiss, David winks as he turns my hat so that the bill is in the back before leaning in and sealing our promises to each other. I am so happy in this moment that I can almost forget that I'm dying. Almost.

I wonder if David is able to forget just for a few minutes. I won't ask him though. This weekend isn't about experiencing one more thing before I die. It's about embracing life and love, hope and family.

Cancer can wait until my appointment on Monday afternoon to be heard.

I Am Cancer

CHAPTER TWELVE

I lose my appetite by Thanksgiving. By Christmas, I'm surviving on a couple cans of nutrition replacement per day. Each day, I'm weaker than the day before, and my body is more painful. But no matter how I feel physically, I've never been happier. When each day counts, each minute counts, you don't have time to waste on thoughts of what you don't have. You are just grateful for one more moment with the people you love.

We have a great last Christmas together. My mother and Frank even come over for a few hours. We laugh until tears run down our faces as we play board games with the kids. Even if

Emmie and Charlotte don't remember the details of our last Christmas together, I'm sure that they will remember the love and laughter shared by all of us.

On New Year's Day, I feel off. It's probably due to all of the holiday celebration excitement, but I can't shake the overwhelming need to confront my mother on the whereabouts of my father. I don't want to though because we've been getting along better than we have since my early teens. As hard as I try to clear my head of this, I just can't. I finally take the cordless phone in the bedroom and call her.

I'm too afraid that I will lose my nerve, so I don't waste time on needless pleasantries. "Hi mom, listen, I have a question for you that may be difficult for you to answer, but I need you to answer me, Okay?"

"You can ask me anything, Tess." Her tone says that she means what she says, but I'm not sure she's prepared for this particular question.

"Do you know where Dad is?"

The line is silent for so long, I almost think that she's disconnected without me noticing. "Mason died less than a year after he left us," she says. "I thought you knew that."

"No, mom. I didn't. You never told me."

More silence. "I know I did. You were really young, so you probably don't remember."

Annoyance crawls up my back. "I'm pretty sure that I'd remember that." I *know* I would have. Every day of my childhood after my dad had left, I waited for his return. I used to watch out the window for his car to pull up in front of the house. Every time we moved, I feared he wouldn't be able to find me when he wanted to. I wondered what I could've done to make him stay away. And now, after thirty years, I find out that he'd been dead this whole time.

"He was in a terrible car accident," she says. "He wasn't the only one that died that day. "We went to his funeral...wait...I think I went alone. I wanted to protect you from…well, you know."

She hadn't protected me though. She hadn't spared me any pain by not taking me to my father's funeral. She'd compounded my grief by not telling me about his death, and then she chose to remember only what she wanted to about the situation—just like she always does. I want to jump through the phone shake her.

"He's buried not too far from your house, actually," she says. "I've put flowers on his grave a few times over the years."

I don't believe her. I don't believe she ever visited my father's grave. She was too busy trying to find his replacement. It takes much effort, but I manage to reel in my anger. It was difficult to forgive my mother when I knew she was sorry, but it's damn near impossible to do it when she's clearly not. I will have to muster the strength to forgive her anyway. I just wish she'd stop giving me reasons to want to avoid her—to want to protect myself from her.

"I got to go, Mom," I say and hang up.

My head is spinning. I didn't expect this. I expected her to say that she had no idea where my father was, even if she actually did. I'd prepared myself to pressure her into telling me what she knew. I never expected to find out that my missing father had never been truly missing.

I Am Cancer

CHAPTER THIRTEEN

David and I walked through the rows of headstones looking for my father's grave. It seemed an impossible task, but I was determined to not give up until I found it. I take my time, reading each headstone and calculating how old each person was when they died. I'm not sure whether I stopped at each one out of respect for the dead or hoping that one day someone else might stumble upon my headstone and wonder about my life.

My favorite headstones were those that were for couples. Those told more about the lives of the people resting there than just dates of their births and deaths. Many of them had the date of their marriage and the names of their children. Those headstones showed that the lives of those buried here touched more than just their own. They lived and loved and left a legacy.

"I think I've found it," David calls from the next row over.

I stand next to him and stare at the plain gray marker. The headstone is smaller than most in this particular cemetery, and it only indicates my father's name, Mason Murdock, and the years of his birth and death. I don't even know my father's birthday, and probably never will now. On this small stone lies the only evidence of his life. Nothing on it speaks of any legacy— of the fact that in his life, he produced someone to carry on his life, who would produce two more people who carry our life in them. It was as if his life hadn't mattered, and it saddens me.

And scares me. He was five years younger than me when he died. He hadn't lived long enough to make much of an impact with his life.

Just like me.

I squat down in front of my father's headstone and run my fingers over his name. "I'm sorry, Dad," I say but am not sure why I'm apologizing.

When I stand, David takes my hand and we resume our meandering through the cemetery. I slow at each double headstone and take in each detail. "They were married for sixty-seven years," I say, wishing that David and I could have as many years together.

A heaviness builds in my chest. It shouldn't be like this. We should have decades left together not months. Or weeks. It's not fair to either of us but especially to David. Nobody should be widowed in their thirties. There is so much of David's life that I won't be around to witness—to share. "I want you to remarry," I say.

"What?"

"I'm serious, David. I want you to have a happy, full life. One filled with love and laughter and not loneliness."

We walk silently for a while until we reach a portion of the cemetery where the markers are spread out more, as if all the empty space is waiting to be filled. One of those spots will probably be filled by me. Although I don't speak this to David, I'm pretty sure he's thinking the same thing.

"You won't have any problem finding someone," I say. "I mean, you didn't before." I stop myself before I say the words *when we were divorced*. We've both avoided talking about that time.

David stops and stares into the distance. The view is spectacular from here, with the mountains in the background and the city in between here and there. The sun is brighter today than typical for this time of year. It's a cold January day, but thankfully, there isn't much wind.

"David."

He shakes his head and says, "I don't want to talk about that."

I stand next to my husband, looking at the mountains but not seeing them. "It wasn't that I wasn't happy back then," I say. "I wasn't anything. I couldn't feel anything. Not happiness or sadness or even anger. I was just empty. Looking back, I don't think I felt like myself since Charlotte was born. Maybe it was just an extended postpartum thing. I wasn't even sure if I wanted to continue living back then. It was as if part of me was sleeping and the other part was just going through the motions of everyday monotony.

"When I suggested we get divorced, I think I was just trying to see if I could feel something. I didn't realize it then though." I glance at David and see him looking at me, and I have to look away.

"I never expected you to leave though," I say. "I thought you'd get angry and yell. At lease

I'd hoped you would have. Then maybe it'd sparked something inside me." I use my free hand to wipe tears from my face. "I couldn't cry back then. Although when you left, my emptiness was filled with tremendous sorrow." I look at my feet. "And regret."

I swallow hard, trying to dislodge the gigantic lump in my throat. "When I saw you with someone else, my ability to feel anger came back. Anger at you, sure, but mostly at myself. And jealousy, so much jealousy. I couldn't believe that I could be replaced so easily. But I didn't have a right to feel jealousy or anger. I was the one who asked for the divorce. I deserved my misery, and I had no problem reminding myself of that over and over.

I realize that I'm shaking. I don't know if it's from the cold, from exhaustion, or from acknowledging my mistakes. "I don't think I fully woke up until I found the first lump. I realized then that I really did want to live. I needed to live, if only to try and make up for all that I'd destroyed."

David pulls me in front of him and wraps his arms around me from behind. I lean into his embrace, and we both just stare for a while.

"They were just fillers, you know." His voice is quiet and melancholy.

"Fillers?"

"God, I hate this," he says. "Those women I dated while we were apart were just fillers."

I stay silent, hoping he will elaborate.

He clears his throat, "I didn't know how to be alone—how to fill all the time I had. I tried working more, but that only made me more miserable. More lonely." He tightens his hold on me. "I missed you and the girls terribly. I wanted so bad to return home to our family. But my pride...I didn't go looking for a replacement. I didn't want anyone else. I was just so...lost. I never should've dated any of them. And I most definitely shouldn't have ever let Emmie and Charlotte see me with any of them."

David steps in front of me, so I can see his face. "I don't want to talk about finding someone else after you're gone. I can't imagine there being anyone else for me."

"I want you to be happy, David," I whisper.

"Just let me savor the time we have left. I won't think of a life without you. I can't."

I slide my arms around his waist and place my head on his chest. "Let's not think about the past or future, I say, "We are here together right now, and that's more than enough." We stand and hold each other for several minutes. "I think this would be a good resting place," I say. "Then when you and the girls visit my gravesite, you can remember this moment."

"Tess, it won't matter where I am, I will always remember this moment."

I tell myself that we still have time. We have the chance to make up for all of the time we wasted apart. I refuse to waste any more of our precious time.

Two days later, I collapse.

I Am Cancer

CHAPTER FOURTEEN

I've been feeling poorly since the day at
the cemetery. I'd thought that it was because I'd
overdone it. My hands and feet feel tingly, and I
can't make it to the bathroom and back without
feeling short of breath. I've been sitting in the
recliner since the girls got home from school. I
know that I need to spend time with them. I force
myself to get up.

As I stand up, everything goes black and
the next thing I know, I'm on the floor between
the couch and the coffee table. "Mommy, are you
okay?" Charlotte yells while sitting on my
stomach.

Cold air rushes past my face, and I hear Emmie outside screaming, "Daddy, Mommy fell!"

Charlotte gets up and runs outside and shrieks, "Mommy's bleeding!"

Am I? I touch my stinging forehead and feel wetness. I must have hit my head on the coffee table. I'm looking at the blood on my fingers when David rushes into the house.

"Oh God, Tess. What happened?"

"I'm not sure," I say. "I was getting out of the recliner one moment and the next I'm here." I try to sit, but I can't budge. "Help me up; I'm stuck."

David lifts me onto the couch and kneels in front of me. My head spins, and I can't take a full breath. The memory of when I was a child and fell off the monkey bars at school rushes to my mind. I'd landed on my back and the air went out of my lungs. The panicky feeling I had trying to catch my breath back then is exactly what I'm feeling now. Only now, every time I try to breathe deeply, it's as if there is no place for the oxygen to go. The pain in my chest increases with every attempt. I fear that I'm dying but don't voice it.

"Emmie, get a wet washcloth for your mother's head. Tess, relax. Try to take a deep breath."

"I can't—" My voice is barely a whisper.

The next several minutes are a blur as David calls 911. I'm not sure I'll make it until the ambulance arrives, but somehow I do. Mrs. Mills offers to keep the kids, so David can ride with me in the ambulance. By the time we reach the hospital, my breathing is still labored but better, so I'm pretty sure that I'll survive this ordeal.

* * * *

I'm in the hospital for three days. The cancer in my lungs has now taken over my ability to maintain the proper level of oxygen in my blood. I will be dependent on artificial, portable oxygen tanks for the remainder of my life. It's funny how I finally have enough hair to hide my illness, but now I have to wear the evidence on my face. At least I could camouflage my baldness with a ball cap. There's nothing I can do about the nasal cannula and tube permanently stationed in plain sight.

Before this ordeal, David didn't have to be aware of my discomfort. Now, he can't look at me without worry etched on his brow. When I was still in the hospital, David tried to convince me that I needed someone with me at all times. "I can't imagine what would have happened had you been alone," he'd said.

But I'm not ready to give up my independence quite yet. I finally agreed to allow my mother or Mrs. Mills to check on me at least twice a day while he worked. David didn't like it, but he'd accepted it.

I wake up in the middle of the night and notice that David's side of the bed is empty. I wait for a few minutes for him to return from the bathroom, but he doesn't appear. I slowly get out of bed, careful to avoid the dizziness from getting up too fast. The hose connected to my large oxygen tank uncoils as I head toward the living room.

I find my husband sitting in the recliner, staring at the lifeless television. I turn on the lamp next to his chair and say, "Why are you sitting in the dark?"

David smiles weakly. "Just thinking."

I can tell that he's been crying. As hard as my illness is on me, it's doubly hard on David. I sit across his lap and put my arm around his shoulders. "Our bed is lonely without you in it," I say.

"I didn't want to keep you awake with all of my tossing and turning."

"I'd rather be kept awake," I say, "than to wake up in the middle of the night alone." I rest my forehead against his.

"I'm sorry," he says.

After several minutes, I say, "I don't think I'm going to make it until May."

"Nope," he says and shakes his head. "I'm not ready to lose you."

I place my hands on each side of his face and say, "You haven't lost me yet." I kiss him on his forehead, then his cheek, and finally his lips. "Come be with me, David."

He shakes his head. "I don't want to hurt you."

His words hit me hard. Rejection rests like bricks in my chest. I feel my face heating up and tears spring to my eyes. David's brows narrow revealing the all-too-familiar worry line on his forehead. He slides one of his arms under my legs and the other around my back. He lifts me easily and says, "There's not much to you."

I look down at my knobby knees and my toothpick thin wrists. It's as if I'm looking at someone else's body. I touch my face. It doesn't feel like me either. Of course, he doesn't want to be with me. Who would? I don't look anything like the woman he married—the woman he desired. I'm just a skeleton with skin. I can't look at him as I say, "I may not look like myself anymore, but I'm still me."

David puts his hand on my cheek, his thumb tracing small circles. He doesn't speak at first. I feel his gaze on my face as he considers what to do with me. He takes a deep breath and lets it out slowly. David gently lifts my chin, so I will look at him. "I see you."

I pull the nasal cannula out of my nose and drop it into my lap. I kiss my husband slowly until I'm out of breath. "Please David. I promise I won't break."

David gives me his crooked smile and places the nasal cannula back in my nose. "You're going to need this." He winks. He stands still cradling me in his arms.

"I can walk."

"I know," he says smiling wide. "But you should save your strength."

I laugh. *This might be the last moment like this.* I push the thought away. I can't afford to waste any more time wallowing.

I Am Cancer

CHAPTER FIFTEEN

I wake with my face pressed against the side of the tent. The voices outside the tent are just far enough away that I cannot make out what they're saying and just close enough to keep me from falling back to sleep. How did David talk me into this? He knows that I hate camping. I press my face more firmly against the fabric in an attempt to find out who's keeping me awake.

"Tess."

The voice is gentle, and I don't recognize it at first. I think it's coming from outside the tent, but as I pull myself out of the deep sleep, I realize that David is gently patting my hand trying to wake me up.

The fogginess of being caught somewhere between wakefulness and asleep is slow to clear. "I had a dream that we were camping in a tent."

"That sounds like a nightmare for you," he chuckles.

"How long have I been asleep?" I ask.

David smiles. "About three and a half hours."

I try to sit up, but David has to help me. I'm going to need that hospital bed the doctor's been trying to force on me sooner than later. I rub my eyes. "Why did you let me sleep so long?"

"You must have needed the rest," he says, as he searches my drawers for something for me to wear. "I have something to show you."

David grabs a clean pair of grey leggings and one of my few pictureless t-shirts. I must not be changing fast enough because David steps in to help. I'm standing in front of the mirror, trying to tame my stubborn bedhead. It was definitely easier when I was bald.

My mother taps on the door and lets herself in. She starts patting at my sticking-up hair. She licks her fingers and rubs my head like she did when I was little, but my hair won't comply with her wishes. "You may have to wet it," she says.

David grabs my hat off of the dresser, places it on my head, and says, "There's no time for that."

My mother starts pinching my cheeks and says, "You're so pale. Maybe a little lipstick will help."

David lifts my hat and plants a kiss on my lips. "Your lips are perfect, let's go."

As I enter the living room, everyone hollers, "Surprise!"

The furniture has been pushed away from the center of the room. Four small tables line one of the walls, each with its own birthday cake and a banner over it wishing one of the four of us a happy birthday. There are balloons and streamers decorating both the living room and kitchen. It isn't until this moment that I realize that it really is my birthday. My last one.

Several of our friends are here. Steph steps forward and gives me a hug. My legs start to give out, and she leads me to my chair.

David says, "When I suggested to the girls that we celebrate their birthdays early along with yours, they insisted that we celebrate mine as well."

I nod. About a week ago, we'd finally explained to the girls that I'm dying. They too young to fully understand what that means. They just know that I will leave one day soon and never return. That night was the most difficult part of this whole cancer thing—it was by far the most difficult night of my life.

David has thought of everything. There are party hats and games for the children. The girls open a few small gifts before David reveals the large dollhouse that we'd talked about buying them as a combined gift. The dollhouse comes in about 1000 pieces. I'm usually the one to put together items like this, but I know that I'm too weak for that. My stepfather and Andrew volunteer for the task. As I watch them pull out all of the parts and look at the instructions, I remember the last thing that I've put together for Emmie and Charlotte—the last thing I'll ever put together for them.

The swing set. David had helped me with that about a month before we separated. I followed the instructions while he did all of the heavy lifting. I'd like to say that we made a good team that day, but that was far from the truth.

"Are you finished yet?" Charlotte asks the men for at least the tenth time. David decides to distract them with a dance party. I sit and watch as my husband takes turns spinning our daughters around and around as they screech with laughter.

He's going to do a great job raising them without me. I know it's not something that he wants to do, but he'll do it. Our girls are so lucky to have him.

As am I.

"Come on, Mom," Emmie says, and I join them in the middle of our living room. David gathers us all in his arms and we all sway slowly back and forth despite the upbeat tempo of the song playing. I don't want this moment to end and I hope beyond hope that somehow Emmie and Charlotte will remember it too.

The girls insist that we sing Happy Birthday four times, once for each of us. After we eat cake and ice cream, David leans next to my ear and says that he wants to take me somewhere. I'm not sure that I want to leave, but Steph and my mother have the girls occupied playing a board game, and I know they will be fine for an hour or so without us.

* * * * *

Of all the places David could be taking me to on my birthday, I didn't expect the cemetery. I'm relieved to see that he's brought my wheelchair. We stop at my dad's grave first and then continue on to the hill beyond most of the graves. He takes me to the spot where we'd talked weeks ago. Only this time it's not a bare spot of grass. This time it is marked with a headstone—our headstone.

Mine and David's.

I swallow the lump in my throat and say, "But, what if you get married again?"

"Tess, I told you I can't imagine marrying anyone else. And, even if I do, you are the mother of my children. My place of rest is next to you."

I grab his hand and pull myself out of my wheelchair. "You're too young to be alone for the rest of your life, and you might have other children."

"I won't," he says simply.

I kneel down in front of our headstone and trace the letters with my fingers: David Michael Peterson—Tess Marie Peterson.

Between our names are two wedding rings with the date of our first marriage. Across the bottom, it reads: Proud parents of Emmie Marie and Charlotte Anne. David kneels beside me."

"Thank you, David," I say. "You have no idea what a relief it is to know—" I don't finish my sentence. I don't have to.

As we drive home from the cemetery, I'm not thinking about dying of cancer. I'm thinking about how grateful I am that, because of my cancer, David and I found each other again. If it took dying of cancer to accomplish that, it has been worth it.

CHAPTER SIXTEEN

I'm in the tent more hours of the day than I am out of it. I've come to realize that this tent is the in-between place, and the fabric of the tent is what separates me from the world beyond this one. The voices are still out there just beyond my ability to hear what they are speaking about. I catch individual words or phrases like *it's okay* or *let go* or simply *come*. I'm hearing my name more frequently from the other side, and sometimes it's difficult to tell whether I'm being called from the other side or this one. I can see light from outside the tent, so I know that the fabric is becoming thinner.

"Tess," a voice murmurs. It takes a few moments for me to recognize that it's David. "The girls are here."

It takes effort, but I manage to pull myself from the tent and back into my own body. I hold my breath for a moment as I adjust to the increased pain being in my body brings. I take a deep breath and open my eyes.

At first, my family is just three individual pieces of colorful light. My vision isn't blurry exactly; it's more like I'm seeing beyond the physical—as if I'm seeing their souls. My sight adjusts, and I smile when I recognize that Emmie and Charlotte are wearing the dresses that they'd worn to our wedding a few months ago. "Hi," I rasp.

The girls don't respond at first. Their eyes are saucers of fear, and I wish that I had the strength to take them in my arms. "It's okay," David says.

"Hi, Mommy," Emmie says. Her bottom lip quivers. I'm not sure if she is holding back tears because I look so awful or whether it had something to do with the conversation that must've taken place while I was out.

"You two look beautiful," I say and pat the bed on both sides of me. David lifts each of my daughters to sit on the bed beside me. "Help me sit up."

David pushes the button on the hospital bed that lifts my head until I'm somewhere between lying down and sitting up. "Come cuddle with me," I say, and both girls take their familiar spots leaning against my shoulders while I wrap my stiff arms around them.

David encourages the girls to tell me about school and dance classes. I try to respond as best as I can but am having a difficult time following the conversation. "Did you hear that, Mommy," Charlotte says.

"Yes, I did. That's really something," I say not really knowing what the something is. "I'm sorry. I'm just so tired these days." I wince as I try to adjust my position.

"It's about time for Mommy's medicine. Remember when I told you that the medicine Mommy has to take makes here extra sleepy?"

The girls nod.

"When I give it to her, she'll probably fall asleep pretty fast, so if you have anything else you want to tell Mommy, you should do it now."

Emmie puts her arms around my neck and says, "I love you, Mommy."

"I love you too, baby, more than you can ever know."

"You're the best mommy in the whole world," Charlotte says, hugging me tight.

I hold both of my girls tight as we all sob, and I wonder if this will be the last time we see each other. Of course, it is. Otherwise, David wouldn't have dressed them up so much.

"Girls," David says, "I think your mom would love to hear that song you learned at Sunday school. I'm going to give Mommy her medicine, then you should sing to her."

Morphine always makes entering the tent easier. Usually I welcome this, but this time, I want to stay with my girls a little longer.

As my eyelids droop shut, Emmie and Charlotte start to sing:

> Rest in me when you are weary,
> Rest in me when you are burdened,
> Rest in me when you are afraid,
> Take my yoke upon you and learn from me,
> For I am gentle, and you will find rest for your soul.

"Keep singing," I say, and they start again.

From a distance I hear the voices from beyond the tent joining the song. As I return to the tent, the heavenly voices become louder, but somehow Emmie's and Charlotte's voices remain the most prominent. When the song eventually ends, I'm barely aware of David lifting the girls from my bed.

I'm fully in the tent now. It's brighter in here. I notice that there is a slight opening in the fabric now. I investigate it to find a hidden zipper keeping the fabric closed. I inch it down a little farther, so I can see what's beyond. All I can see is color—vibrant color. It's like nothing that I've ever seen. It's not just more beautiful or bright. It's just more.

I can make out more of what the heavenly voices are saying now. The excitement in their voices is growing. It's as if they are awaiting some great event, some long-anticipated event, one that's about to happen. I can't help but be caught up in their delight. At first, I don't understand why they are all so enthusiastic, but then I grasp it.

They're waiting for my arrival.

I flee the tent, back into my own body and force myself to open my eyes. My mother is sitting next to my bed, holding my hand. She looks beyond weary. She looks as if she has aged twenty years in the past few months. It occurs to me that even though she went over fifteen years without seeing or speaking to me that this time it's different. Our previous separation had a temporary feel to it, as if we had plenty of time to repair our broken relationship.

This time it's permanent—utterly and totally permanent.

"Mom," I say.

"Oh, Tess," my mother says. "I need to get David."

"Wait, Mom." My tongue feels thick and stiff.

"But, I promised him that I would get him as soon as you woke up. He didn't want to leave you, but he really needed to rest."

I squeeze her hand. "I love you," I say, hoping she can understand my garbled speech.

Tears fall rapidly down my mother's face. "I'm so sorry, Tess, for everything."

I believe her. "I forgive," I take a deep breath, "you."

She throws her arms around me and sobs. She speaks into my neck, but the only words I can understand are "A mother should never outlive her child."

"David," I say, and she jerks herself upright.

"I have always loved you more than anyone else in my life."

I pat her hand. "I know," I say, and she leaves to get David.

I thought my mother looked exhausted, but David is in far worse shape than she is. Cancer may be killing my body, but it's destroying my husband. He kisses my forehead.

"Hold me," I say.

David lowers the side of my hospital bed and crawls in next to me. I hold my breath as he pulls me into his arms, so he won't know how much it hurts to be moved like this. He gently rubs my back and says, "It's okay to let go, Tess. We'll be fine."

It's clear that he speaks these words because they are the right words to say not because he means them. I tighten my grip on him.

I ease myself back into the tent and unzip the zipper a little more. I stick my head out through the opening and for a moment, I see clearly. It's too much, so I pull my head back in.

I hear the words "It's okay, Tess," spoken from both worlds.

For the first time, I recognize a gentle pull from the other world. It had been there before, unnoticed, but now it's stronger. I resist for a while, but then I return to the zipper. I lower the zipper far enough open so that my whole body can fit through. I ease myself out while holding tightly to the tent's opening.

I'm floating as if I'm in the ocean or in space. I relax there, just being. The pull from the other world is stronger than the one holding me in this one. Heavenly music flows from the voices on this side of the tent. "Come, Tess," one of them say.

I realize that out here, I'm no longer in pain. I can't feel my body anymore; I can't feel David, and it scares me. I thrust myself back into the tent all the way back to my body. I gasp as the pain from my ailing body hits me like a sledgehammer.

David jerks awake and resumes rubbing my back. "It's okay, Tess. We'll be fine," he begins, but then his voice breaks into sobs. His body jerks with each raking sob, and all at once I see it.

We are one.

Our souls are connected like two tightly grasped hands. When I leave this world, when I pry myself from him, I will be taking half of my husband with me. I don't want to do it; I don't want to leave. I can't bear the thought of ripping him in two. But, I know that I don't have a choice.

David's sobs ease, and he lets out a deep breath. With the breath, I feel his soul's grip on mine lessen. We lie here, holding each other, wishing we had more time.

But I know that my time in this world is short. As much as I want to stay, my body is just too weary and broken to survive here. I long for the feeling of being outside the tent—the lack of pain, the weightlessness, the gentle pull toward the welcoming voices.

"I love you, Tess. You've suffered enough. The girls will be okay. I'm okay." He leans forward, kisses my forehead, and says right into my ear, "Go with God."

And, I let go